For Anna,
Catherine and Blythe,
who inspired me to persist, and
for Eli and Georgia, my every day inspiration.
— L.W.
For my parents, Hank and Carol, and
husband Ross, with love and appreciation.
You've helped make my dreams
a reality.
— S.C.

Library of Congress Cataloging-in-Publication Data is available.
Library of Congress Catalog Card Number 2010936998

ISBN 978-0-9829938-1-1

13 12 11 10 09      1 2 3 4 5 6 7 8 9 10

Printed in Canada
First edition 2010

Little Pickle Press LLC
PO Box 983
Belvedere, CA 94920

Please visit us at www.littlepicklepress.com.

# Sofia's Dream

By Land Wilson

Illustrated by Sue Cornelison

Little Pickle Press

Sofia was a thoughtful girl,
　　　Who called the moon her giant pearl.

　　　　As nights passed and the moon would grow,
　　　　　　She marveled at its opal glow.

One bright night in a dreamy state,
Sofia heard a sound quite late.
As she peeked around at all her toys,
She wondered which one made a noise.

When a beam drew her gaze up high,
She saw a face that winked its eye.

"Hello down there," the moon sang out.
"I hoped to find you peeping out."
"I didn't know the moon could talk."
"Of course I can, I just can't walk."

"I'm very pleased to meet you, Moon.
Can we talk again real soon?"
"If any night I light the sky,
Just say hello and I'll say hi."

From this night on a friendship grew
Into a bond both strong and true.

When her friend was only half in view,
    Sofia asked, "Where's the rest of you?"
If he was just a crescent moon,
    She knew that he might vanish soon.

Then one time when the moon seemed blue,
    She noticed that his face was too.
"Excuse me, Moon, what bothers you?
    There must be something I can do."

"You need to come and visit me,
For there is something you must see."
"But you are up there far away!
"I'm here on Earth. I have no way."

"My dear friend let me share with you,
Something special that you can do.
Tomorrow night, when you're asleep,
Dream that you take a giant leap."

So she closed her eyes. In her mind,
Sofia left the Earth behind.

When she reached the moon in space,
She asked about his gloomy face.
"Now, my friend, that you are here,
I'll show you what it is I fear.
Take a close look at Earth with me,
Then tell me what it is you see."

"There's giant swirls of white and blue.
It's like a marble in our view.
I see such a beautiful place,
Surrounded by the black of space."

"Your Mother Earth is where you live.
    She is my closest relative,
Also home for nature's wonder,
    Now she's saddened by real plunder."

"With dirty waters, land and air,
    It looks as though she's in despair.
Her people seem so unaware,
    That what Earth needs is better care."

"Why would some want to hurt the place
    Important to my human race?
She is the only home I know,
    Where living things can breathe and grow."

"I see now why you feel so sad.
    An upset mother's very bad.
I wish you were not feeling blue.
    Please tell me, Moon, what should we do?"

"You all must think of Earth each day,
And care for her in every way.
Learn more about what you can do,
To help the Earth and all of you."

"The things you do and what you say,
Will make a difference every day.
Aim high with everything you do,
Then you'll inspire others, too."

"Thank you, Moon,
for the thoughts you share.
It makes good sense. We need to care!
More people need to visit you,
So they can see your point of view."

When Sofia woke up from her dream,
Her cares were different, so it seemed.
Part of the work she pledged to do,
Was passing on these words to you:

"One of these nights, I hope quite soon,
Dream that you leap up to the moon.
There you will find a wise old friend,
Who has a point of view to lend."

"Once you see from this distant view,
Awareness may come over you.
By far your gift of greatest worth,
Is our dear home, this planet Earth."

# Our Mission

Little Pickle Press is dedicated to helping parents and educators cultivate conscious, responsible little people by stimulating explorations of the meaningful topics of their generation through a variety of media, technologies, and techniques.

## Little Pickle Press
### Environmental Benefits Statement

**Knightkote Matte** (FSC), by SMART Papers is made with 40% post-consumer waste fiber and 50% total recycled fiber, elemental chlorine-free pulps, in acid-free and chlorine-free manufacturing conditions. It represents an exceptional combination of responsible natural resource utilization and expertly crafted matte-coated papers for the highest quality, environmentally-conscious printing results that meet and exceed archival standards.

**Little Pickle Press saved the following resources by using Knightkote Matte paper:**

| trees | wastewater | energy | solid waste | greenhouse gases |
|---|---|---|---|---|
| **51** | **19,649** | **17** | **1,725** | **5,244** |
| Fully Grown | Gallons | Million BTUs | Pounds | Pounds |

Calculations based on research by Environmental Defense Fund and other members of the Paper Task Force.

**MOHAWK** windpower

We print and distribute our materials in an environmentally-friendly manner, using recycled paper, soy inks, and green packaging.

Little Pickle Press

www.littlepicklepress.com

## About the Author

Land Wilson was born and raised in Marin County, California. He has been drawn to many forms of artistic expression, including theater, arts management, and art restoration. His interest in writing began in college, and over the course of his long career in business, writing has become his favorite form of personal artistic expression. Land developed a deep appreciation for nature as a child, and his interest in environmental protection was his motivation for writing *Sofia's Dream*. Land lives in San Rafael, California, with his wife and two children.

## About the Illustrator

Sue Cornelison grew up in Libertyville, Illinois. After earning her BFA in Art Studio and Art Education from Drake University, she traveled to Florence, Italy, to further her art studies at The International School of Studio Arts. While raising a family of six children with her husband, Ross, a jazz musician, she taught high school art and pursued her love of art, design, and illustration. She has illustrated many book covers and enjoys writing and illustrating books for children.